A Gift from Rolling Readers Volunteer

Joy

To a Very Special Child

Michael

Rolling Readers USA
PO Box 4827, San Diego, CA 92164–4827

ROLLING READERS USA ®

A 20th Century Fox Presentation

ANASTASIA™

A Don Bluth/Gary Goldman Film

Princess Anastasia

by Jan Carr

illustrated by the Thompson Brothers

HarperActive™

A Division of HarperCollins*Publishers*

A 20th Century Fox Presentation

ANASTASIA™

Princess Anastasia

*I*f I were a princess,
I'd dress up in a gown.
My skirts would rustle on the stairs.
I'd wear a jeweled crown.

If I were a princess,
I'd curtsy at the ball.
The orchestra would play a waltz.
I'd dance around the hall.

*S*ome think I *am* a princess.
They teach me how to bow.
They say, "Speak up!" "Sit straight!" "Stand tall!"
"Walk slowly!" "Curtsy now!"

Oh, why can't I remember
what happened in the past?
And what about this key I wear?
I'd like to know at last.

To find if I'm a princess,
I journey very far.

I come by train.

I come by boat.

I travel in a car!

Perhaps I *was* a princess,
and had a music box
that played a soothing lullaby,
a song this key unlocks.

The music sounds familiar.
Somehow I know the song.
It proves I'm Anastasia.
I start to sing along.

And now that I'm a princess,
I do not have to roam.
At last I've found my grandmama.
At last I've found my home.